MOUSE AND OWL

STORY
JOAN HOFFMAN

ILLUSTRATIONS
JOHN SANDFORD

COLORING
GAIL L. SUESS

It is a quiet night.
The moon is bright.

Owl sees a mouse
run out of his house.

"What a good dinner he will be.
I'll just wait here in this tree."

Mouse sees Owl waiting there.
That big bird gives him
quite a scare.

Mouse hunts for his food at night.
But he must hide
from hungry Owl's sight.

For Mouse, any grain will do.
He eats seeds, leaves, and roots, too.

13

"What can I do? Where can I go?
Owl is watching me, I know."

Mouse thinks of food.
He sniffs the air.
He knows he can't go.
Not with Owl up there!

That big bird is much too quick
for tiny Mouse to trick.

Owl just sits and stares.
He knows that Mouse is
out there, somewhere.

Suddenly the trees begin to shake
as a thunderstorm begins to break.

Mouse does not know why,
but now there is no light
in the dark, dark sky.

"Now is the time for me to go.
I must not be slow, I know!"

Quickly he runs into his house,
before the owl can see the mouse.

It will soon be light. Will Mouse
and Owl find food tonight?